Shout Daisy
SHOUT!

Jane Simmons

ORCHARD BOOKS

To Ruby and Denis who never shout

Other great Daisy books

Come On, Daisy!
Daisy and the Egg
Daisy and the Beastie
Daisy's Hide and Seek
Daisy Says Coo!
Daisy's Day Out
Daisy's Favourite Things
Go To Sleep, Daisy

Orchard Books
96 Leonard Street, London EC2A 4XD
Orchard Books Australia
Unit 31/56 O'Riordan Street, Alexandria, NSW 2015
First published in Great Britain in 2002
ISBN 1 84121 547 3
Copyright © Jane Simmons 2002
The right of Jane Simmons to be identified as the author
and illustrator of this work has been
asserted by her in accordance with the
Copyright, Designs and Patents Act, 1988.
A CIP catalogue record for this book is available from the British Library
1 3 5 7 9 10 8 6 4 2
Printed in Singapore

Daisy loved visiting Auntie Lily's, there was always so much to play with.

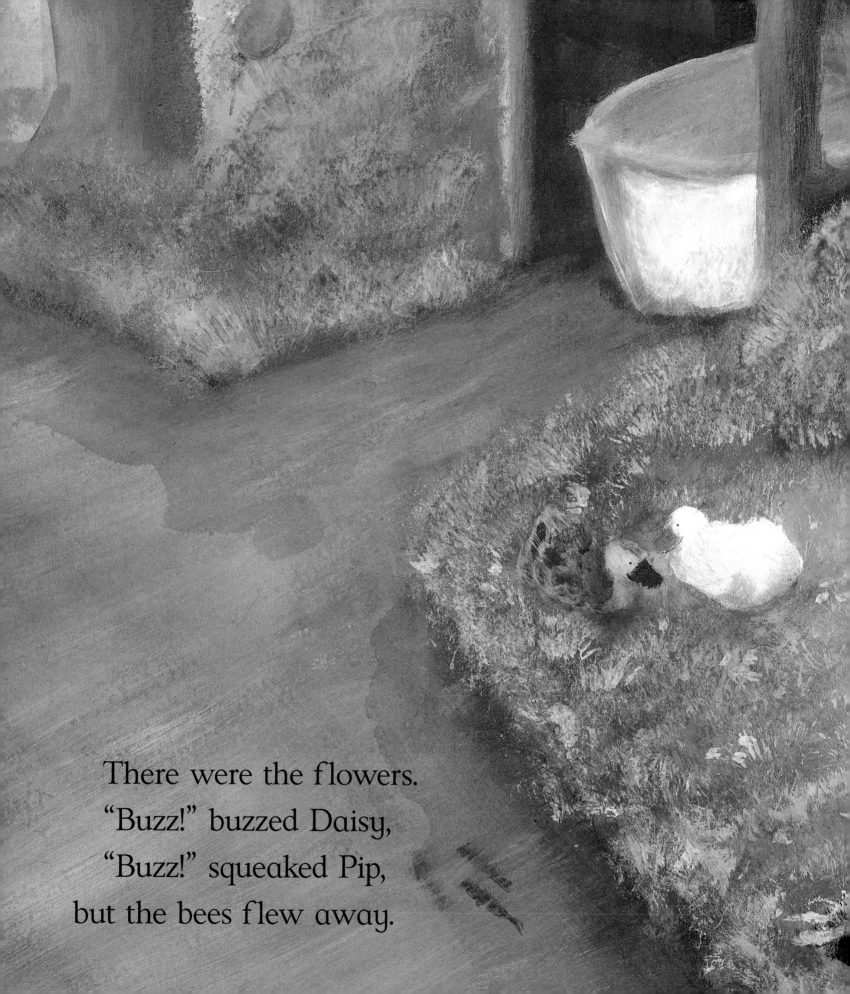

There were the flowers.
"Buzz!" buzzed Daisy,
"Buzz!" squeaked Pip,
but the bees flew away.

And there was the bird table.
"Tweet!" squawked Daisy,
"Squeak!" squeaked Pip, but
the birds took off too.
"Oh dear," said Auntie Lily.
"Try being a bit quieter," said Mamma Duck.

Daisy tried, but she wasn't quiet for long.

eek

eek

. . . and the mice ran away.

splish

splosh

. . . and the fish went too.

And even the balloon
floated up, up and away.

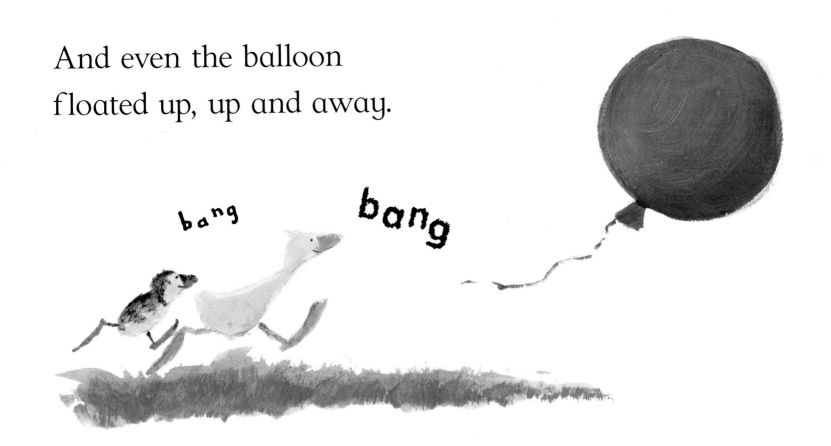

bang   bang

Then there was nothing
left to play with.

"Come on," said Auntie Lily,
"I know a perfect place for
being noisy!" and they all set off.

Everyone was quacking so loudly.
"Now you can make as much
noise as you like!" said Auntie Lily.

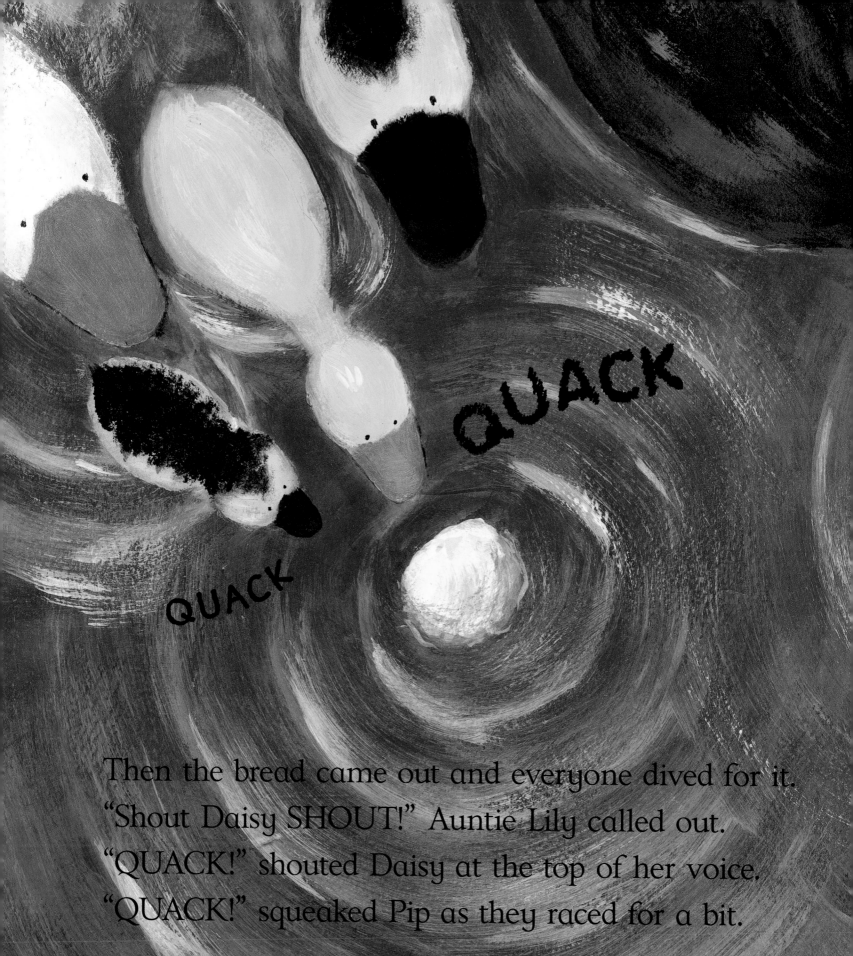

QUACK

QUACK

QUACK

Then the bread came out and everyone dived for it.
"Shout Daisy SHOUT!" Auntie Lily called out.
"QUACK!" shouted Daisy at the top of her voice.
"QUACK!" squeaked Pip as they raced for a bit.

They got it,

and pulled

and pulled.

It broke in two.

They softened it

and munched
it down.

Suddenly there were ducks
everywhere, everyone was quacking!
"Daisy! Pip!" shouted Mamma.

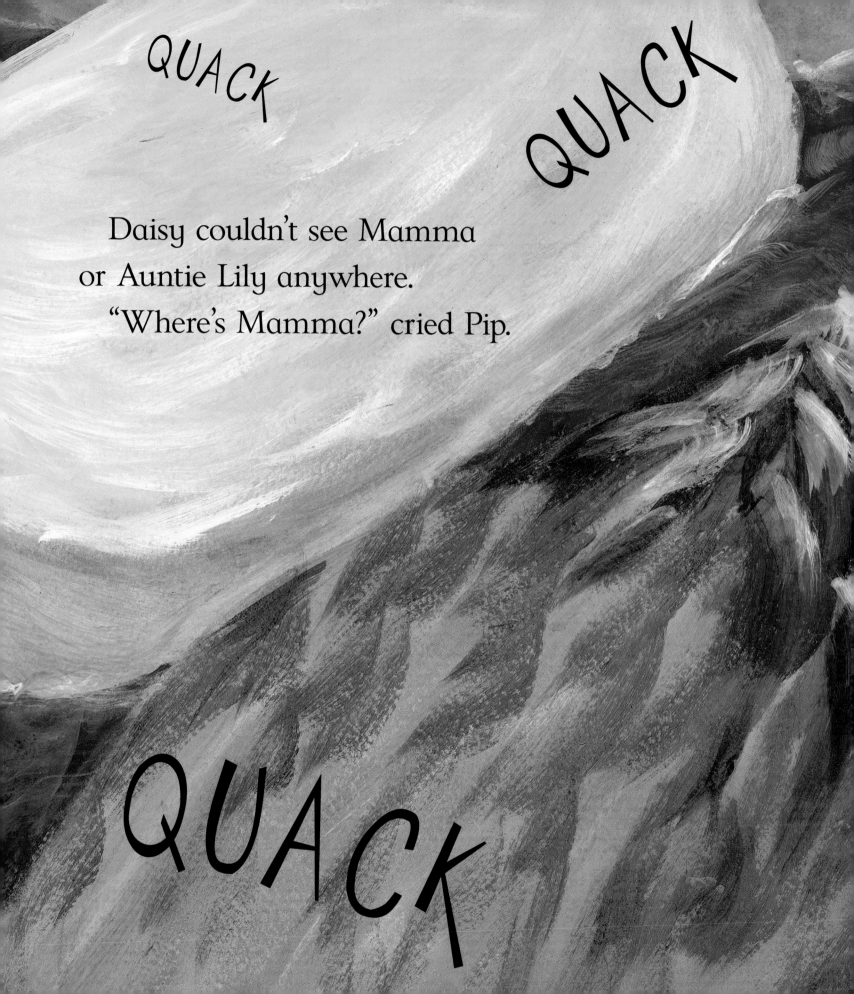

QUACK

QUACK

Daisy couldn't see Mamma
or Auntie Lily anywhere.
"Where's Mamma?" cried Pip.

QUACK

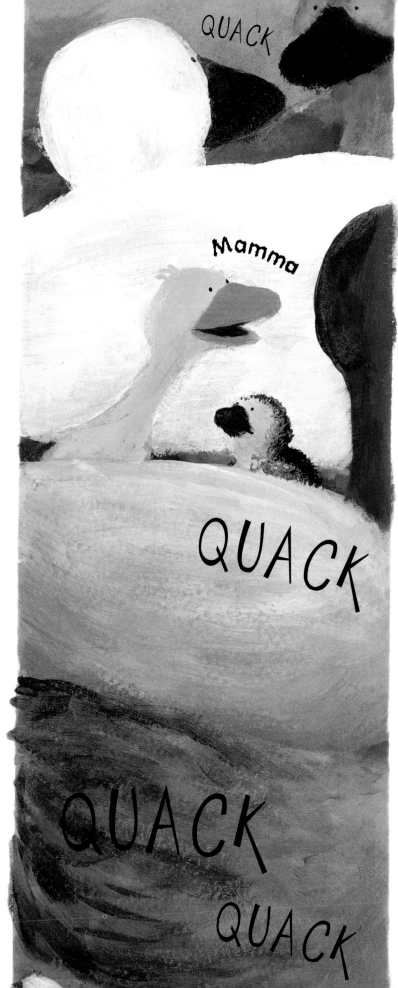

But all the
quacking was
too loud.

"Mamma!"
cried Pip.
"She can't hear us,"
said Daisy.

QUACK

QUACK

QUACK

More bread came and everyone was pushing and shoving and shouting.

Everything went quiet.

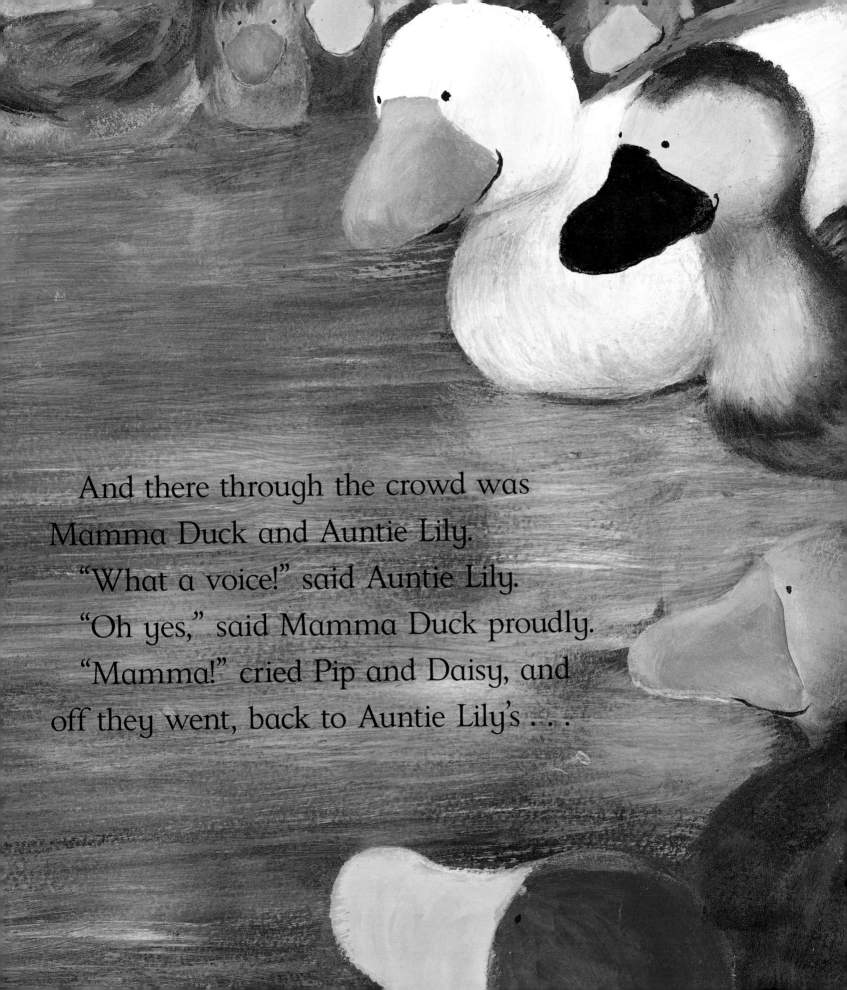

And there through the crowd was
Mamma Duck and Auntie Lily.
"What a voice!" said Auntie Lily.
"Oh yes," said Mamma Duck proudly.
"Mamma!" cried Pip and Daisy, and
off they went, back to Auntie Lily's . . .

. . . for a very, very quiet afternoon.